This book was bought with
money gifted to the
nursery by the Deyell
family, in memory of their
late father, Bertie Deyell
of Semblister, Bixter.

First published in hardback in Great Britain by Andersen Press Ltd in 2001
First published in paperback by Collins Picture Books in 2002

3 5 7 9 10 8 6 4 2
ISBN: 0-00-712635-2

Collins Picture Books is an imprint of the Children's Division, part of HarperCollins Publishers Ltd.
Text and illustrations copyright © Colin McNaughton 2001
The author/illustrator asserts the moral right to be identified as the author/illustrator of the work.
A CIP catalogue record for this title is available from the British Library.

The HarperCollins website address is: www.fireandwater.com

Printed in Hong Kong

Colin McNaughton

Oomph!

Collins

An imprint of HarperCollinsPublishers

We're all going on a summer holiday… sang Preston's mum and dad as they headed off for a week at the seaside.

I'm going, too!

"Just think of it," said Preston.
"Sunshine, sea, sand…"
"…And sausages!"
said Mister Wolf.

At last they arrived.
During the journey, Preston
was only sick twice,

and he only said,
"Are we nearly there, yet?"
thirty-seven times.

Preston slipped on his swimsuit,
slapped on his sunhat,
slopped on his sunscreen
and set off across the sand.
Suddenly!

"Why don't you look where
you're going?" said the little girl.
"Sorry," said Preston.
"Are you all right?"

"I suppose so," said the little
girl. "How about you?"
"My nose hurts," said Preston.

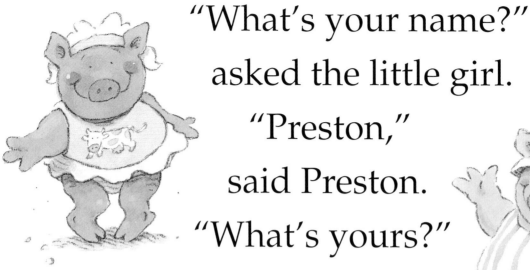

"What's your name?"
asked the little girl.
"Preston,"
said Preston.
"What's yours?"
"Maxine," said Maxine.
"But everyone calls me
Max. You're fat."
"Thank you," said Preston.
"You're rather plump yourself.
I like your swimsuit."
"Thank you,"
said Max,
and she gave
a little
twirl.

"How's your nose?" said Max.

"It hurts," said Preston.

"I'll kiss it better!" said Max.

And she did.

Gag!

Caw!

"You're blushing!" said Max.

"Must be sunburn," said Preston.

"You're funny," said Max.

"Let's play," said Preston.

The next day was Sunday...

Preston was up bright
and early to meet Max.
"Let's make sand castles," said Max.
And they did. All day.

Max told Preston her dad was a lifeguard so she spent the whole summer on the beach. "Lucky you!" said Preston.

Big pig!

Hi, Dad!

On Monday they went surfing…

"Wave!" shouted Max.

"Who to?"
shouted Preston.

"You goof!"
laughed Max.

"How's your nose?"

"Tender!"
shouted Preston.

"Kiss it better?"
shouted Max.

"Race you to
the beach!"
shouted Preston.

On Tuesday they dug a hole…

"How's your nose today?" said Max.

"Sore!" said Preston.

"Kiss it better?" said Max.

"Thank you, nurse!" said Preston.

On Wednesday they
explored rock pools…

"Watch out for the
slippery seaweed," said Max.
"Yes," giggled Preston.
"If I slipped I *might* hurt
my nose again…"
"…and I *might* have to kiss it
better again!" giggled Max.

On Thursday they
went sailing…

"I hope you put plenty of
sun cream on your nose,"
said Max. "Otherwise…"
"…You *might* have to kiss
it better!" laughed Preston.

On Friday they went snorkelling…

And on Saturday they said goodbye…

"Come back soon!"
shouted Max.
"Soon as I can!
shouted Preston.
"Preston!" shouted Max.
"Did you know you had
a wolf on your roof rack?"
"Very funny!"
shouted Preston.
"Goodbye, Max.
I'll write
to you!"

'Bye, Preston.

And this is what he wrote…

Dear Max,
I'm back home now
and my nose is
better, thanks to
you (blush blush).
I wish I was still
at the seaside
with you.
I had the best time
ever. Thank you for
being my friend.
I miss you.
Love Preston xxx

Collect all the Preston Pig Stories

Colin McNaughton
Suddenly!
Look behind you, Preston Pig!
0-00-714013-4

Colin McNaughton
GOAL!
Go football crazy with Preston Pig!
0-00-714011-8

Colin McNaughton
BOO!
Surprise! It's Preston Pig!
0-00-714014-2

Colin McNaughton
Oops!
I'm coming to get you, Preston Pig!
0-00-714015-0

Colin McNaughton
Shh!
(Don't Tell Mister Wolf)
A Preston Pig Lift-the-Flap Book
0-00-664715-4

Colin McNaughton
Hmm...
Who's hungry for Preston Pig?
0-00-714012-6

Colin McNaughton
Oomph!
Fall in love with Preston Pig!
0-00-712635-2

Colin McNaughton
little Suddenly!
a Preston Pig toddler book
0-00-713235-2

Colin McNaughton
little Oops!
a Preston Pig toddler book
0-00-713236-0

Colin McNaughton
little Goal!
a Preston Pig toddler book
0-00-713234-4

Colin McNaughton
little Boo!
a Preston Pig toddler book
0-00-713237-9

Colin McNaughton
WHEE!
A Preston Pig TV Story
0-00-712371-X

Colin McNaughton
POOH!
A Preston Pig TV Story
0-00-712370-1

Colin McNaughton
PARP!
A Preston Pig TV Story
0-00-712372-8

Colin McNaughton is one of Britain's most highly-acclaimed picture book talents and a winner of many prestigious awards. His Preston Pig Stories are hugely successful with Preston now starring in his own animated television series on CITV.